THE BEST LOVE

Ever Since The Accident
❧ Book One ❧

Ruth E. Griffin

Studio Griffin
A Publishing Company
www.studiogriffin.net

For information, contact:
Studio Griffin
A Publishing Company
studiogriffin@outlook.com
www.studiogriffin.net

Cover Design by Ruth E. Griffin
Image by © fizkes/Adobe

First Edition

ISBN-13: 978-1-954818-33-0

Library of Congress Control Number: 2017919682

2 3 4 5 6 7 8 9 10

For Mo, my best love

The best love is the one you fell in accidentally. The strongest love is the one you fell in unexpectedly. The truest love is the one you fell in wholeheartedly.

Anonymous

Julieta

FOR A BRIEF MOMENT, JULIETA stopped breathing. Her heart rate slowed down and her head grew light and dizzy, making her feel as though she might pass out.

Julieta was, in fact, fine but this was a common malady in her life that only occurred whenever she was around Alex…

Tall Alex, with the slender, muscular frame…

Handsome Alex, with the grey, soulful eyes…

Beautiful Alex, with the sandy-brown hair, cut short as of lately, just how she liked it…

It didn't help that she saw him almost every day, but even now, as he walked into her home, she couldn't resist admiring him. Nestled comfortably under a blanket, Julieta watched as Sonia, her sister-in-law, greeted Alex and welcomed him into their home. He, in turn, offered her a shy smile and allowed her to kiss his cheek. Manny, Julieta's brother and Sonia's husband, met his friend at the door with a cold beer and a firm handshake. The two of them worked together at a construction company, Manny as the foreman and Alex as a laborer. They had met years ago when Julieta was too young to do anything about her crush, but she had recently celebrated her twenty-second birthday. She was old enough to date him and fulfill his every desire, should he ever ask.

But it was all wishful thinking on her part: Alex had never shown interest in her. And even if he did, her over-protective brother would never allow it. Manny had spent her teenaged years warning her about men who were nothing but trouble to good girls like her. Men, like Alex, who had spent time in prison and wanted only one thing from women: sex. Now that she was older and aware of her own sexuality, the thought was actually quite appealing. And to be frank, his past didn't bother her at all—everyone deserved second chances. But she also knew she would never convince either of them that a relationship was worth pursuing.

Still, it didn't stop her from fantasizing, which in turn *stopped* her from breathing.

Julieta released the breath she had been holding and let her body resume its normal functions. She slid down into the couch as Manny and Alex proceeded past the living room to the back deck where her brother had the grill going. Neither offered a glance in her direction. She was invisible to all but Sonia, who approached her with a warm smile. Everything about the woman was beautiful. She had big brown eyes, flawless olive skin, full supple lips, and the perfect hourglass figure. Julieta was a troll compared to her, with light brown skin, black hair and dull eyes—just like her brother. But if there was an upside, it was that Sonia had a soft spot in her heart for both of them. The woman was a saint to deal with Manny, whose explosive temper rivaled that of a volcanic eruption. But also with Julieta, who had to depend more on her following the accident.

With a soft touch, Sonia brushed Julieta's hair back and kissed her forehead.

"Can I get you anything, *mamita*?"

Julieta shook her head.

"I'm good."

"Let me know if you do need something; dinner will be ready shortly," she added before heading back to the kitchen.

Julieta turned her attention back to the television. She tried to remember what she was watching before Alex walked in, but she was a hopeless case. As long as he was in the house, she wouldn't be able to concentrate.

You seriously need to grow up and stop crushing on your brother's friend, she thought to herself.

Julieta decided to put Alex out of her thoughts. She grabbed the remote and channel-surfed instead. She knew she ought to be looking at the class schedule Manny picked up, but school no longer appealed to her. All because of the accident.

Sonia had picked her up from the community college that afternoon. They had two cars between the three of them and Julieta had to depend on her sister-in-law for a ride. It was raining; and neither woman saw the pick-up truck barreling towards them on Julieta's side. The vehicle rammed them, causing their car to overturn several times. Sonia escaped with little injury, but Julieta was not so fortunate: a metal bar pierced her leg. She lost a lot of blood because of it and had to receive multiple transfusions. At one point, she even went into cardiac arrest and flatlined. But she made it. She was alive, and this was something she didn't take lightly.

Which was why she wasn't certain about college anymore. She had missed the latter part of the previous semester but now she had the opportunity to retake the classes and get back on track. Yet, she hesitated. Yes, she understood getting an education was vital to her future, but the truth was she didn't know what she was going to school for anymore. What were her goals? What did she want to do? Could she postpone going for a year while she figured stuff out? And if she never did, could she be happy settling for what everyone expected of her?

"Hey, Jules."

Alex plopped down on the seat beside her, a plate in each hand. That he called her by a nickname was as much as a surprise as his choice to sit so close to her. She pulled the blanket closer to her chin and forced herself to breathe.

"Hey," she managed, though it was hardly coherent or intelligible.

He passed a plate to her.

"Sonia said to bring this to you."

Julieta pulled her arms out from under the blanket and accepted it.

"Thanks."

She set the plate in front of her, and tried to focus on anything but Alex, but she was too aware of his presence to relax or eat.

Dammit, girl, grow up.

"What're you watching?" he asked, casually.

Julieta tried to answer him, she really did, but no words escaped her lips. She just stared at him.

Idiot!

Then Sonia and Manny entered the living room, sparing her from further embarrassment. They carried plates and drinks with them. They would be eating dinner in the living room, as much on her behalf as there was a game on that Manny wanted to watch. Sonia handed Julieta a glass of water and sat down on the couch across from her.

"What's this crap?" Manny asked, snatching the remote from her.

Not caring for his sense of entitlement, she exclaimed, "Hey, I was watching that!"

He stopped and turned to her, his arm extended, finger ready to hit the button and change the channel.

"Oh, yeah, what were you watching?"

Julieta glanced at the television and was surprised to see she had it on a children's channel.

"Uh..."

"Yeah, that's what I thought."

"You're a jerk."

"And you're a baby."

He flipped through the channels until he found the game he was looking for.

"Not everyone in the room wants to watch that," she insisted.

"So, leave," he retorted as he took a bite of his food, his eyes glued to the game.

Sonia swatted him on the leg in chastisement.

"Manny! Be nice."

"What?" he asked without looking up. The ball was intercepted, and Manny yelled in frustration.

Julieta sighed. Loudly.

Manny noticed.

"Why don't you go fill out that paperwork for school? You're supposed to start classes next week," he remarked. Even though his comment was in the form of a question, Julieta knew it wasn't a suggestion. He wanted her to leave.

"You don't have to be so snarky," Julieta shot back.

He turned to her, his expression hard—he wasn't playing anymore.

"*Ey*, I know you got hurt and all, but it's time to get back to school." He spoke in a 'fatherly' tone, trying to impart whatever wisdom he thought was appropriate. The problem was that she was not *his* child. She wasn't even *a* child anymore, so he could keep whatever advice he had.

"I don't want to go back yet," she said, firmly.

"You want to be like me? No college degree, stuck working construction because you can't get anything better? You're too smart for that," he continued. "You have to think about your future."

Julieta rolled her eyes.

"You never cared before."

"Yeah, well, I care now."

"Why? Because you're not getting a return on your investment?"

Sonia cut in.

"You two need to take this somewhere else."

"Julieta needs to understand she can't throw her life away. She's going back to school," Manny argued.

"No, I'm not. I get to decide what I want. This is *my* life," Julieta retorted.

"Not while you're living in *my* house."

"Then I'll move."

"Where are you going to go? Who's going to take you in like that? You're a cripple."

Julieta blushed at her brother's insensitivity. She had scars that ran the length of her leg and had to walk with a cane. So yeah, she was a cripple, but Manny had no right to say so, especially in front of Alex.

"Then again, maybe that's a good thing," he added. "I don't have to worry about you getting knocked up."

"*Basta!*" Sonia yelled. She was usually the level-headed one, but even she was losing patience now. "This is ridiculous. You two fight like children."

Manny ignored her and directed his next comment at Julieta.

"I'm gonna say this and I'm done." His voice was grave and low. "You're a smart girl and I won't let you throw that away. You're going to register for your classes and finish college and that's all there is to it."

Julieta didn't dare argue. Manny was ten years older than her and had spent the past decade parenting her into adulthood. He was the man of the house; and as a good Latina, it was her 'duty' to respect and obey the man's authority. She didn't like it, but there was nothing else she could do.

"Understood?" he added, making eye contact with her to assure there was no misunderstanding.

"Yes," Julieta replied through clenched teeth.

Silence followed. The only sound in the room now came from the television; and though Manny's team scored, there was no celebration.

"I can take her," Alex suddenly volunteered.

Everyone looked up at him. Julieta stopped breathing again, but for a different reason. While Alex had given her rides in the past, he hadn't done so since the accident. If he took her tomorrow, he would see her hobbling about on her cane. As much as she wanted to be around him, she didn't want him to see her like that. She prayed Manny would say no, as it was apparent her fate was in his hands and not hers.

"You told me to take the afternoon off tomorrow. I'm not doing nothing, I could come by and take her," Alex said, then added, "If you're good with that."

Julieta groaned when she saw Manny considering it.

"Works for me," he finally said with a shrug of his shoulder. Then he turned back to the game, the conversation over.

THERE WAS A knock on the door. With an exaggerated sigh, Julieta set down her coffee mug. Alex was right on time.

Dammit.

She picked up her cane and stood up, careful not to place her full weight on her leg. Then she lumbered from the kitchen to the front door where she caught Alex in midair as he prepared to knock again. He dropped his hand and gave her a smile. For a moment, Julieta lost her breath as she took in his beauty...

Then she remembered why he was there and mentally kicked herself for losing it over a smile. This morning, Alex was the enemy and she needed to treat him as such. Yes, she knew she was being childish, but he was the one who volunteered to take her to get registered. She might have found a way out of it had he said nothing at all.

"You don't have to do this, you know," she told him, as she leaned on the door.

He shrugged his shoulders.

"I didn't have anything else to do."

"Well, how about we go somewhere else and just say we did this?" Julieta suggested.

Alex frowned and shook his head.

"I don't think that's a good idea."

"Why not?"

"Your brother—"

Julieta cut him off, annoyed that he would bring Manny into this.

"My brother is not in charge of me."

"No, but he is bigger than me," Alex thoughtfully replied.

He had her there.

"Fine," Julieta mumbled, then turned back to the kitchen. "Let me get my purse."

"You want any help?" he asked.

"Nope," she said, curtly. She took her time as she placed her mug in the sink, cut off the lights and hung her purse over her shoulder. Unable to stall any longer, Julieta returned to the living room, where Alex was watching her with amusement. Her attitude soured even more.

Outside, Julieta shuffled her way to Alex's car. It was a classic, an older model sports vehicle with a manual transmission, original parts and one visible flaw—it was low to the ground. It was never a problem before the accident. Now? Julieta stood awkwardly by the passenger side debating how to get in without injuring herself, or more importantly, looking like a complete idiot.

Alex had opened the door and was waiting patiently on her. He opened his mouth to offer his assistance again, but Julieta gave him a sharp look, silencing him. She wasn't quite sure what he was going to say, but whatever it was would have cost her dignity. Determined to do this on her own, Julieta leaned on her cane for support and placed her bad leg in first, guiding herself into the seat, butt first. She could feel Alex's eyes on her and imagined how ridiculous she looked.

Once she settled into the seat, Alex shut the door and walked around to the driver's side.

"Last chance," she offered once he was in, though she was under no illusion he would actually take her up on the offer. Indeed, Alex only smiled; then he started the car, and they were off. The ride was a quiet one; Julieta refused to indulge in conversation while she was still pouting. And since Alex was a man of few words anyway, nothing was lost in the silence.

When they arrived at the college, Alex again offered to help her, but Julieta waved him off and did the best she could to stand up by herself. Inside the main building, Alex waited in the hallway while Julieta completed her registration. Her advisor asked her question after question about the accident. Julieta hid her annoyance and kept her answers short and concise. They filled out all the appropriate paperwork and reviewed the classes she would be taking. An hour later, Julieta emerged from the office with her schedule in hand, no worse for wear, but still annoyed.

Alex jumped to his feet when he saw her, his hands buried deep inside his pant pockets, a sympathetic expression on his face. Julieta's attitude relaxed a little bit when she saw this.

"You done?" he asked, moving so close to her, she could smell his cologne. It was a strong, wonderful, masculine scent—everything she thought he was.

"Ah, yeah," she replied.

"I know it's late, but you wanna grab some lunch?" Alex asked, his hand on her back, guiding her towards the door.

Julieta's heart beat a little harder and her breath became a little shallower. She wasn't hungry, but she was happy to spend the next hour or so with Alex.

"Sure," she replied coolly.

In the car, Julieta suggested an old diner on the outskirt of town. Alex was happy to comply, until they pulled up to the parking lot. It was a rundown, hole-in-the-wall; but Julieta assured him the food was worth it.

"*Papi* would bring us here all time, always said the same thing: never judge the inside by what the outside looks like."

Alex reluctantly agreed.

Inside, the atmosphere was quaint; and though the furniture was old, the place was clean, and the staff was friendly. After sitting down, a short, round waitress with a genuine smile and a cheery voice approached them and took their order.

"Chili fries for you, honey," she repeated as she pointed to Julieta, "And for the handsome gentleman, a cheeseburger and fries."

They nodded.

"I'll be right back with your drinks."

She returned quickly, as promised, and let them know their food would be ready shortly before leaving again. Julieta unwrapped her straw and sipped on her diet cola.

"So why don't you want to go back to school?" Alex asked her after a moment of silence between them.

The question surprised Julieta. He was the first and only person to ask her this.

She set down her cup.

"Honestly? I'm not in a hurry to get back to doing more of the same stuff I was doing before—school and work and homework and school and work and homework. I know I'm blessed to have those things, and I'm not trying to be ungrateful or anything, but after the accident…"

Her voice trailed off. She knew what she wanted, but it sounded cliché, stupid even. People everywhere, every day survived worse than what she experienced. The fact that she walked away should have been reason enough to appreciate what she had. But it wasn't and she wasn't certain Alex would understand. Even still, when she saw him gazing at her expectantly, Julieta continued.

"After the accident, everything now seems pointless. I know this could have been worse, but right now, I don't know why I'd be going back to school. Does that make sense?"

He nodded and asked, "Have you told Manny this?"

She shook her head.

"What for? He wouldn't get it."

"He's your brother."

Julieta laughed, contentiously.

"You *obviously* never grew up in a Latin household. As the man of the house, whatever he says, goes. And since he paid for school, I have no choice but to go back and finish, whether I want to or not."

"I'm sure he's just looking out for your best interest."

"I know. But I want to be able to make decisions for myself, you know? I am an adult."

"Being grown-up is sometimes overrated, trust me."

She did. Still...

"I can't be a kid all my life."

"I'm sure Manny will see the woman you've grown up to be."

The words came out of his mouth casually, almost nonchalantly. To her ears, though, they sounded calculated, sexy even. Julieta's face warmed at the thought. Then she realized she was staring at him, and he was staring back at her...but not with the same expression she bore. His eyebrows were slightly raised, as if he was pondering the nature of her thoughts.

Their waitress arrived then, saving Julieta from having to explain herself. She turned her attention to the woman as she set their respective plates down on the table in front of them.

"You all enjoy now," she said with a smile and a wink, and left them to their meal.

Julieta focused on her food, her face still warm. For a split second, she considered telling Alex how she felt about him, but since the probability that he would requite the affection was non-existent, she dismissed the thought. Julieta picked up her fork and made a hole in the middle of her fries. She filled the hole with a mountain of ketchup and began eating.

"So, what are you going to do?" Alex asked.

Julieta stopped chewing, surprised yet again: she didn't think he would continue the conversation. She thought about it for a second, then cheekily responded, "It doesn't matter anymore. I'm enrolled now, thanks to you."

Alex smiled sheepishly at her but didn't apologize.

"I'm kidding," she said. "I don't know. Do what I've been doing, I guess. Eventually maybe I'll get a backbone and stand up to my brother."

"Give yourself more credit than that. You've gotten this far; you'll figure out what to do."

If only, she thought, pushing back thoughts of him. She smiled nonetheless and said, "Thanks."

WHEN THEY ARRIVED at Julieta's home, Alex put his car into park and shut it off. Without a word, he exited the vehicle and walked over to her side. He was going to walk her to the door, and Julieta had no problem with that.

Alex opened the door for her, grabbed her books and offered her his hand. She accepted his help this time, allowing him to balance her weight as she stepped out of the car. Then he moved aside and gave her the space she needed to stand up and start towards the house. He kept pace with her, until she reached the front door. Then he shifted back so that she could unlock the door. Once she was in, he followed her into the kitchen, where she set her purse on the table and turned to him. Alex continued holding her books, awkwardly.

"You can set them on the table," she said.

He did so, then returned to his original spot, seemingly waiting for something. Feeling awkward, Julieta offered, "You want something to drink?"

Alex shook his head.

She nodded, unsure of what else to say.

"How's your leg?" he asked her.

"I'm okay. I can't be on it too long, but today wasn't too bad."

This time, Alex was the one who nodded.

Another awkward silence followed. Alex was over a head taller than her, which made a face-to-face conversation difficult. So, Julieta looked around the room, wishing she was more outgoing. Figuring he was probably looking for a way to say goodbye, she cleared her throat and said, "Thanks for today."

"Even if you didn't want to go?" he asked, the humor plain in his voice.

She smiled.

"Your company made the excursion bearable," she ventured, finding enough courage in her to flirt, even if it was innocently.

"Just bearable?"

"Just," she said, then without giving herself enough time to reconsider her actions, she leaned onto her cane, rose onto her toes and kissed him on the cheek. If ever there was a time a kiss could be justified, this was it and she was going to take advantage of it. His face was clean-shaven, and he smelled so wonderful, she almost lost her footing. But she did not; and as quickly as she kissed him, she withdrew and dropped back down to her feet, proud of her thievery.

Julieta didn't look up immediately, but when she did make eye contact, she saw Alex lean down and kiss her. Not on the cheek, like she did him, but on her mouth. With lips so warm and supple, Julieta forgot how to react. That she couldn't breathe was a given. She was also paralyzed, unable to do anything except watch as Alex touched his lips to hers. All without any reaction from her.

Then he ended the kiss and stood upright once again. Julieta still didn't know what to do, even as the realization of his actions hit her.

Alex kissed you! Oh my God, Alex just kissed you…

Why though? As much as she wanted this, she had to know why he did what he did. And though the words were contrary to everything in her, she managed to ask, "Why did you do that?"

Alex thoughtfully considered her question.

"I care about you."

'Care' was such a generic word though.

"Care, like how?"

He chuckled.

"I like you," he clarified.

Julieta still wasn't satisfied.

"Why now? I mean, we've known each other for...a while. What happened?"

"The accident," he said simply.

Julieta cringed. Everything lately was a result of the accident and she hated it.

"I know we haven't meant much to each other, but that changed after the accident. How I see you, how I feel about you. The possibility of losing you, then the pride I felt watching you find the courage and strength to rebound the way you did. I know it may feel sudden to you, but this has been my life for the last few months. I didn't know if you would feel the same for me, but I had to take a chance. I had to know."

Julieta was dumbstruck once again. His words were magical, everything she wanted to hear. Yet she hesitated. She had become so accustomed to viewing him as unattainable, she didn't know how to see him as anything else. Worse yet, every objection Manny could possibly offer played in her head.

He's an ex-convict.

He's playing you.

He only wants sex.

He'll ruin your future.

But as she searched his face, she could see he was being sincere. And she wanted that, she wanted what he was offering her—himself.

"I feel the same way," she finally said, softly, shyly.

Alex smiled and leaned down towards her again. Still, she hesitated.

"What about Manny?" she asked.

Alex stood back up.

"What about him?"

"He's not going to give us his blessing."

She was loath to admit it, especially to him, because she didn't see Alex as Manny did. But given her brother's prejudice towards 'bad boys', she knew he was the biggest obstacle they would face.

Alex sighed, but he didn't lose the mirth that had filled his eyes moments earlier.

"He's your brother, so I'll respect whatever you want to do."

His response only endeared him to her more and made her realize this was what she was searching for: the opportunity to live her life. On her terms. She loved Manny and she wanted his approval, even if he was sexist and pig-headed sometimes. But she wanted Alex more. She loved him and wanted to find out what their future held.

Love? Really? she scolded herself. She could admit she cared for him deeply, but was it love? Or did it even matter now that Alex felt something for her?

If you say it out loud, it will. You'll scare him away.

She couldn't do that. She didn't know exactly what would happen between them, but she had waited this long, and she wasn't going to ruin it. Eventually she would admit she had a crush on him. But not for a while. Maybe even years. If ever.

"Jules?"

Again, the nickname. Her breath instinctively became a little bit shallower, but today she had more than her fantasies to sustain her. Which meant she had to answer him.

"No, I want this," she said. "I want you."

Alex leaned into her once more and without waiting to see if she had anything else to say, he kissed her. Julieta was ready for him this time and she responded with all the passion she had saved up for him. He moved his arm behind her and pulled her in closer, the contours of his body pressing against hers. She felt his tongue on her lip and she opened her mouth for him. A tingle ran through her as their tongues met, making her feel like she could float away. The feeling was familiar, yet so new.

Julieta dropped her cane and wrapped her arms around his neck. Her leg started to give out, but Alex picked her up and cradled her in his arms. Still kissing her, he carried her to her bedroom, where he gently lay her down on her bed. He caressed her body, his touch loving, reverent and attentive. He took his time, lavishing her with his veneration. Alex was a quiet lover and Julieta found this more attractive than all the other features that had captured her attention all these years.

Then he pulled away from her, dragged his shirt over his head and revealed a magnificently crafted torso, covered in a patchwork of large, gothic tattoos. Julieta became breathless again, admiring the sight he was offering her. Which became more obvious as he unbuckled his pants. Without thinking twice about it, she slid back to make room for both of them. Then she sat up when Alex grabbed the bottom of her shirt and removed it. He placed his knee on the bed, in the space between her legs and leaned into her, over her, his lips touching hers again. To her surprise, Alex wasn't as gentle as he had been moments earlier. As his tongue made inroads in her mouth, his hand wandered over her body, his grip hard as he pulled her to him and onto their sides. He dropped on the bed and brought her leg up over his, running his hand up and down her thigh. A moan escaped her lips as his assault on her senses continued. She could feel him, hard and ready for her. Everything he did felt good and right; but it was too much on her leg. A stinging pain shot through her body, and she cried out.

Alex sat up away from her.

"I'm sorry," he cried. "I'm sorry."

Julieta propped herself up on her elbows, her leg throbbing.

"No, it's okay," she replied, her eyes shut tightly. Or it would be, she told herself, once the pain subsided. Every now and then she would wear herself out or turn the wrong way and her body would react like this. She had grown accustomed to it because she had no choice, but sometimes she wondered if this was her new normal.

Julieta clenched her fists and released them, willing the pain to go away. She eased her breathing and finally opened her eyes to see Alex watching her with concern and guilt.

"I'm okay," she assured him.

The expression on his face told her he wasn't as convinced she was. Julieta knew she had killed the mood, but now she felt like she had ruined any chance she had with him. "Really. This happens sometimes. It's okay. You didn't do anything. I probably just strained myself today. We can keep going."

"I don't want to hurt you," he said.

"You won't."

Alex stared at her pensively. He couldn't mask the guilt on his face, but he also couldn't hide the care he professed for her either. The sincerity in his eyes was unmistakable.

Emboldened by it, Julieta sat up and kissed him on the lips. He seemed to hesitate at first, but as she deepened the kiss, he responded. Julieta opened her mouth for him and found his tongue waiting.

She laid back onto the bed, pulling him with her. Body to body, skin to skin, she ran her hands up and down his arms, tracing the tattoo closest to her. She relished the feel of his skin beneath her fingertips and listened to the rhythm of his heart, now beating in concert with hers.

LOST IN THE moment, Julieta was barely able to process the next words she heard.

"What the hell?"

Manny!

Before she could react, her brother had pulled Alex off her and onto the floor, where he began to punch him. She screamed, scared for Alex. Manny had a fierce temper and had done violent things in his youth because of it. As his sister, the worst she got was an attitude and a raised voice. But this was something else. It was frightening, disturbing and beyond her control.

Without thought to her leg, or the fact that she was only half dressed, Julieta scrambled off the bed and towards her brother. "Manny, stop!"

Sonia appeared at the door.

"Manuel!" she yelled.

But he wouldn't stop. Manny continued hitting Alex, one punch after another. Alex didn't fight back. He only threw his arms over his head in an attempt to protect himself and pleaded for the older man to stop.

"I bring you into my house and you try to have sex with my little sister?"

"Stop!" Julieta begged.

Sonia tried to stop Manny, but in his rage, he shoved her back and she fell to the floor.

"What the hell gave you the idea you're good enough for her?"

There was a gash on Alex's cheek, and his nose was bleeding. His left eye was beginning to bruise, and his handsome face was now battered. With tears streaking down her face, Julieta tried to get between them. Her leg gave out though and she found herself next to Alex, dodging punches. Sonia pulled her back, so she wouldn't get hurt.

"What the hell made you think she even wanted you?" Manny persisted, his fist red with Alex's blood.

"Stop! Stop!" Alex cried, but the older man didn't listen. He continued to hit him again and again, until Alex's face was almost unrecognizable.

"What made you even think she wanted you? *Eh*? Answer me!"

"She did," Alex finally admitted, his voice strained, tepid.

Manny stopped, his arm caught in midair. He gazed at Julieta, his rage now directed at her. But she was too baffled to react. What did Alex mean, *she did*? Was he implying she had started their affair? With the kiss she gave him on the cheek?

"You gonna tell me Julieta started this?" Manny asked, turning back to Alex, ready to pummel him again. The younger man pushed himself away from her brother. His face was red, though it was hard to tell if it was from the blood or the beating. What was not hard to see was the expression of loathing and regret he bore. He stared at Julieta, his expression apologetic.

"Well?" Manny yelled, his patience growing thin.

"At the hospital…" –the words seemed to stick in his throat– "you told me that you loved me and wanted to be with me."

Julieta's eyes widened as her heart began pounding in her chest. She felt hot and was painfully aware that all eyes were on her.

"No, I didn't," she insisted. She didn't remember much about the accident, but she was certain she hadn't volunteered something so personal.

Alex avoided her gaze as he explained, "It was after your first surgery. Manny had gone to Sonia's room and a nurse, I guess figuring I was family, took me to the ICU. You woke up and when you saw me, that's when you said… what you said."

Julieta was horrified. Obviously, she had had a reaction to the anesthetics, but even that knowledge didn't lessen the blow of her actions. She had told Alex she loved him. She had revealed her crush to him. How could she do that?

"I'm…," Alex said, but nothing else followed. He had no words to offer, no apology to give, no shame to feel. She wasn't sure what she expected, but suddenly, she felt angry. How could he embarrass her like that? What had he hoped to gain? To stop Manny from beating him? Or to get her to act on the things she told him? Her humiliation turned to rage.

Sonia squeezed her shoulders, but Julieta pulled away from her.

"So, you thought you'd do what? Take advantage of me?"

Alex shook his head.

"Julieta, no—"

She didn't let him finish.

"You took what I said and used it for an easy lay?"

She pulled herself up and stood over him, adrenaline now coursing through her body. He recoiled from her as if she might pick up where her brother left off and pleaded, "Listen, please—"

"Did you get a kick out of it, watching as I fell for your guise? I bet you couldn't wait to get me back here, knowing I'd worship you," she spewed as tears stung her eyes and clouded her vision.

"Jules, please…" he begged, reaching out to her.

Hearing him call her by that name only fueled her rage. Julieta slapped him.

Hard.

"Go to hell," she exclaimed. Then turned her wrath on Manny, who was equally guilty in her eyes. "You too. Both of you go to hell!"

Manny frowned.

"What did I do?"

"What right do you have to walk into my bedroom? I don't need you checking up on me or rescuing me."

"Obviously you do, if this is the kind of sleaze you invite into your bed," he exclaimed, pointing to Alex.

"That's what I'm talking about. You act like you have to control everything and make decisions for me like I'm incapable of it. In case you haven't noticed, I'm not a kid anymore. I'm a woman."

Manny scoffed at her.

"Then stand up and take responsibility for your life. Live without my support. See what happens." His tone was harsh, his words like daggers piercing her skin. "Go on, stand up on that bum leg of yours and see how far you get."

"Manuel!" Sonia warned.

Julieta had had enough though. She stumbled out of the room to the bathroom, where she locked the door, slid to the floor, and cried.

Alex

ALEX HAD SCREWED UP—AGAIN. IT seemed he was always in trouble; this time, though, it had burned not only him, but Julieta as well. It broke him to see her run from the room the way she did, but there was nothing he could do about it now. She was gone; and he was left behind at the mercy of her brother. Alex had seen Manny's temper in past but was never on the receiving end of it.

Until today.

Neither said anything as Sonia ran after Julieta; and now that the adrenaline had slowed its course, Alex could feel pain surging through his body. Especially his face. It was white hot and tender; and he could taste blood on his lip.

Manny shifted his stance and turned back to him. Alex braced himself for another pounding, but the man only growled, "Get the hell out of my house."

He wouldn't even look at him.

Unwilling to give Manny a chance to change his mind, Alex quickly stood, grabbed his shirt, and exited Julieta's room. Now in the hallway, he saw Sonia trying to talk to Julieta through the bathroom door. She glanced up at him briefly. Unlike Manny, though, her expression was one of sympathy and pity. Alex stopped, thinking to explain himself, but knew better than to do so with Manny nearby. Sonia might understand what really happened, but he wouldn't. And so, Alex left.

It was early evening. The sun was still up, but it would be dark soon. Normally, he and Manny would still be at work, but because he had the day off, Alex had planned a few hours alone with Julieta. It didn't end that way though. Maybe if he had started earlier, if he took her home after registering, talked to her, waited...

Alex sighed as he dropped into his car and slammed the door shut. He pulled down the visor and stared into the mirror. The bleeding had slowed, but his face still felt like it was on fire. His eye was half-shut, and his cheek was turning purple. He tried wiping the blood from around the side of his mouth and nose, but he was unsuccessful, leaving his face a hodge-podge of colors and bruises. Alex gave up trying. Instead, he closed the visor, started his car, and drove home to his one-bedroom apartment. It was on the bad side of town, but with a prison record and no credit, it was all he could get when he moved to the area years ago. It served its purpose though and that's all he needed. The sun now setting, Alex parked his car under a streetlight and climbed the stairs to his apartment. His neighbor, an older man with a paunch and little hair on his head, was out on the deck smoking.

"What happened to your face?"

"Nothing," Alex mumbled and let himself into his place. He tossed his keys on the table and made his way to the bathroom to clean up. He found a washcloth and ran it under some warm water to wash his face. His skin was tender and caused him pain as he cleaned up all remnants of blood, leaving only the bruises. He had been in fights before, but this was the worst beating he got.

Because you wouldn't fight back.

Regardless of what Manny did to him, Alex couldn't hit him. Out of respect, but mostly brotherly love.

A lot of good it did him.

Alex grabbed some aspirin and downed the pills without water. Then he dropped onto his unmade bed and turned the television on. He flipped through the channels, but nothing caught his attention. Desperate for a distraction, he decided to eat something. There was nothing in his fridge though. Only a loaf of bread and some condiments, reminding him how often he was over at Manny's house.

This is pathetic, Alex thought. He grabbed his keys and left.

"WHAT THE HELL happened to your face?"

After driving around for some time, Alex finally stopped at a bar he often frequented. Or had frequented in the past. It had been a while since he had been there; and except for the loud drunk at the bar who inquired about his face, it seemed like the best place to be right now. Alex ignored him and headed to the corner where he could drink in peace. After ordering a beer, he propped his head on his palm and stared at the television above the bar.

"Hey stranger."

Alex looked up to see a short blonde approaching him. It was Lisa, the secretary to the owner of the construction company he worked at. He had dated her for a while, but things didn't work out between them, and they split up. They didn't see that much of each other, except at the office, or this bar, which was probably why he stopped going there. She was a nice person and all; she just wasn't what he wanted.

Not that he knew what he wanted…

That's not true. You know exactly what you want. It's just not going to happen now.

Lisa smiled when he met her gaze, but quickly frowned when she saw his face.

"What happened to you?" she asked, taking a seat next to him. She reached for him, concern spelled out across her face, but Alex shook his head and moved away from her touch. When he didn't respond, Lisa said, "I hope the other guy looks worse."

Still, he said nothing. The last thing he wanted was for her to know was who kicked his ass. Everyone on the job site would be talking about it by the time he showed up for work on Monday.

Lisa waved the bartender over and placed her order.

"So?" she asked. "You're not going to give Lisa the dirt?"

Alex cringed. He hated when she referred to herself in third person.

"There's nothing to tell," he finally said, taking a swig from his beer.

"If you say so," Lisa said, unconvinced. But seeing that he wasn't going to talk, she changed the subject. "Did you hear what happened to Gary? He fell off the scaffolding, shattered his pelvis. They had to stop work."

She continued filling him in on the events of the day, but Alex stopped listening after a while. He wanted to be alone; but more than that, he wanted to forget. So, when the bartender came back with Lisa's order, he requested another beer. Then another. And another. With each beer that followed, he waited for the numbness to set in, so he could forget Julieta. It never happened though. The more he drank, the more he remembered: how she looked, how she felt, how she tasted. And worst yet was the knowledge that she believed he had preyed on her when the situation was the exact opposite.

Alex had been with Manny the night of the accident. He was waiting on the older man to finish up, so he could take him home. The two carpooled, since Manny's car was in the shop at the time. That's when the call came in: Sonia and Julieta had been in a car accident. They rushed to the hospital but had to wait as both women were in the emergency room. During the time that followed, they exchanged no words, only anxious thoughts, nervous pacing and desperate prayers. Alex was never very religious, but there was something in him that day that sought a higher power, if only for the sake of his friend. He had lost many people in his short life, and he didn't wish that upon anyone else, much less Manny.

Then the news came: Sonia had miraculously escaped with a few bruises and scrapes. Julieta, however, had sustained massive injuries to her leg. She had lost a lot of blood and had to have emergency surgery.

While Manny went to his wife's side, Alex chose to stay in the waiting room. Time passed and eventually the doctor came out with news about Julieta: they had stopped the bleeding and she was stable. But she had a long road to recovery ahead of her. A nurse escorted him to Julieta's room. Alone with her in the intensive care unit, Alex was shocked to see her so broken. She bore cuts and bruises all over her body, while her leg was wrapped up and resting on a pillow following her surgery. He had never seen her so fragile, and his heart broke for her.

Alex sat with her for a while before she stirred. He thought to get the nurse, but then Julieta turned to him, eyes barely open, and groaned.

"Julieta?"

She seemed to recognize his voice.

"Alex?" she said, her speech, low, raspy. She opened her eyes and when she saw him, she repeated his name. Then she made her confession of love, words so incredible, so *incredulous*, he couldn't do or say anything.

Julieta closed her eyes, still mumbling, and was back asleep. Alex knew her admission stemmed from a reaction to the anesthetics coursing through her body. But words like that didn't just come out nowhere. Was it possible she really felt like that about him? Why else would she say it? And if it was true, why would she love him, of all people? What the hell could a smart girl like her want with someone like him? What did he have to offer? He destroyed everything he touched.

Alex didn't mention her confession to anyone, especially Julieta. Instead, he watched her. And as she began her recovery in the weeks that followed, he started seeing her in a different light. She didn't complain or let the situation get the best of her; she pushed through what needed to be done. Subsequent surgeries were successful; and with the help of physical therapy, she regained use of her leg. In all his life, he had never met a stronger woman.

And a woman she was. Julieta had always been 'Manny's little sister', invisible to him. Now, though, she was something else, something more. She was smart and ambitious, but also beautiful, with dark, expressive eyes, and a warm, inviting smile.

He had never considered her appearance before, but looking at her now, he couldn't deny his attraction to her. This new view of her forced Alex to take stock of his life. He had distanced himself from his past when he met Manny, but now that he knew Julieta saw something in him worth caring for, he wanted to try harder, he wanted to be better—for her. Alex didn't understand everything that was happening, but the longer he was around Julieta, the more he wanted her.

So, when Manny told Julieta to register for class, Alex jumped at the chance to be alone with her. How else could he know if everything he was feeling was real or not? And when he finally mustered up the courage to kiss her, it was like a spark shot through him, leaving him wanting more—of Julieta, of them, of what they could be.

Then Alex had to screw everything up. He should have kept his dick in his pants, should have waited, gone slower, stopped. He should have told her the truth, told her how he really felt about her. But he did none of those things and now he was sitting in a bar alone, trying to forget. Ultimately, he could live with his mistakes. The one thing he couldn't live with was the knowledge that Julieta thought less of him.

THE BANGING ON the wall woke Alex up. It seemed to be coming from everywhere, irritating every nerve in his body. But as he regained consciousness, he realized it was all in his head—the pounding, but also the nausea, the aching, and the pain. He was suffering the effects of a hangover; and between it and the swelling of his face, Alex felt terrible.

He dragged his eyes open and focused on the object in front of him. It was tan and fuzzy, with a streak of pink around the middle. What was he looking at? Alex concentrated until his vision became clear.

It was a teddy bear.

He frowned. Where was he?

Alex forced himself to sit up. The room spun out of control and his stomach threatened to spill its contents. He leaned forward against his legs, until everything settled down. Or settled down as much as could be expected. Alex sat up again and looked around him. He was sitting on a full-size bed, covered in a pink, frilly duvet, surrounded by plush bears of all shapes and sizes. The room appeared to belong a teenage girl, which made Alex uncomfortable. Especially when he saw he was only wearing his boxers and socks.

Where the hell was he?

The door opened, and Lisa walked in, carrying a cup of coffee. She was wearing a sleep t-shirt, nothing else.

"Good morning, sunshine," Lisa said, as she sat on the bed next to him, her leg touching his.

Alex groaned. He had intentionally drunk to forget; and forget he did—most of the evening after the first few drinks. Apparently though he had compounded one mistake with another. How could he do something like this after pursuing Julieta? Even if she didn't want him anymore, he still wanted to believe he could be someone who was worthy of her love.

"Here," Lisa said, holding out the cup to him, along with four pills.

He hesitated.

"Relax. You were too drunk to do anything last night, including drive home," she said with amusement. "Besides you kept talking about Julieta. Isn't that Manny's sister?"

The company had rallied behind Manny after the accident, collecting and donating funds to assist him with the hospital bills. It was touching to see their support, but it also now meant Alex couldn't keep his business to himself. Lisa only knew about Julieta because of the accident. And it wasn't like the name itself was a common one. Lisa would put two and two together, then let everyone know why Manny had beat him. Which would probably piss the man off even more, so that he would be inspired to finish the job he started.

Alex sighed. His life was over. There was no point denying the truth.

"Yeah," he muttered.

"I didn't know you and her—"

"We aren't."

"That's not what it sounded like."

Alex gazed up at her. He wasn't sure he wanted to know what he said.

"You need to stop beating yourself up…or at least stop letting others do that for you,"

Lisa admonished him. "You're not exactly a push-over, so if you didn't fight back, then you obviously like this girl a lot. Don't give up so easily."

"Look at my face. What else should I have done?"

She shrugged her shoulders.

"I don't know. Maybe that goes with the territory—dealing with the over-protective older brother," she said, a hint of humor in her voice.

"I don't think it matters anymore," he sighed.

"I think it matters to you," Lisa insisted. When he didn't argue, she shook her head and said, "Here." She opened his hand and dropped the pills into it. He looked at them for a moment, before popping them into his mouth and chasing them down with a sip of coffee.

"Look, I know I talk a lot, but you need to trust me, okay? If you're serious about Julieta, you need to tell her. Everything this time."

Alex sighed. He knew she was trying to help, but he wasn't feeling it. Then he realized what she said. He frowned and asked, "What exactly did I say last night?"

Lisa smiled knowingly at him, but she didn't respond. She stood up, pointed to the chair in the corner, currently occupied by a plush bear the size of a small child and said, "Your clothes are over there. I washed them for you." Then she exited the room, closing the door behind her.

Alex swallowed the rest of his coffee, then sat for a while until he felt functional again. Slowly, he stood up and meandered to the chair. He grabbed his pants and put them on. Then he left the sanctuary of the bedroom to find a bathroom. He did his business and washed up. His head was still hurting, and he had a sour taste in his mouth, but it was all par for course for a night out drinking.

Alex returned to the bedroom and finished getting dressed. Sluggish steps took him to the kitchen where he placed the empty mug in the sink. Lisa was seated at the table, reading a book. She looked up at him and asked, "You want something to eat? I could make you a sandwich or something."

Alex shook his head. The thought of eating was enough to make him want to vomit.

"I'm good."

"Do you want a ride to your car? We had to leave it at the bar."

"No, I'll walk. The air will do me some good."

Lisa nodded. An awkward silence followed, as Alex struggled to find the right words to express his gratitude. Eventually, he said, "Thanks."

He was terrible when it came to communicating with women.

"Talk to her, Alex," she reiterated.

He nodded; and that was the end of their conversation. Alex waited a moment longer before he turned and left.

Outside, Alex started his walk back to the bar, which was a few miles from Lisa's place. He took steady steps towards his destination, pushing himself to continue, even though his body wanted to quit. He kept his head down and eyes on the ground below him, avoiding eye contact with the people around him. He told himself it was because the neighborhood was rough, but really, it was more of a habit, one he developed in prison. It kept him out of trouble then, and now. Except it also allowed him to focus on his thoughts. Like what he was supposed to do now. His first impulse was to let the situation go, and Julieta with it, but that would mean letting her believe he had taken her words and used them for his advantage.

Isn't that what you did?

No, he cared for her.

But you wouldn't have if she hadn't said anything.

He had no answer for that. The truth was he would have continued down the path he was on without her if she had said nothing at all. So, what was it about her words that drew him to her? Fate perhaps? If so, that meant he would have eventually looked past the superficial and been drawn to her. But with his kind of luck, it would have been too late then. She would have moved on and found someone who was truly worthy of her.

Even if this was true, Alex didn't want to give her up. His mind screamed for a second chance. Maybe Lisa was right. He needed to tell Julieta the truth. The entire truth this time.

"WHERE YOU BEEN?"

The neighbor with the paunch was back out on his front deck smoking. Alex wasn't sure he had seen him do anything else.

"Nowhere," Alex muttered and let himself into his apartment. It was exactly how he left it, which wasn't comforting at all, because it was still empty—of family and food. And after walking to his car, then driving home, Alex had found his appetite. He settled for more aspirin and some water instead.

The television was still on, but Alex ignored it as he sat on the edge of his still unmade bed and pulled his phone out of his pocket. Had enough time passed? Should he call Julieta? Would she answer the phone? Would she even talk to him? What about Monday? He and Manny usually carpooled together—would the man talk to him then? Or would he...what? Hit him again? Cuss him out? Ignore him?

Even at his worst, Alex couldn't remember feeling this low, or insecure.

Deciding it best to call rather than spend the rest of the day worrying, Alex dialed the number he knew so well. It rang once. Twice. Three times. By the fourth and final ring, Alex's heart was pounding so hard it hurt. The answering machine kicked in, but he didn't know what to say, so he hung up.

He turned his attention back to the television and tried to get lost in the programming. He was unable to muster up interest though and eventually got up and showered. He called Julieta again, but like before, no one picked up. He hung up without leaving a message.

Alex popped more aspirin and went back to bed, finding solace in the darkness. He hardly slept that night though and was up at daylight. He waited until mid-morning to call Julieta again and this time, he left a message for her. He didn't explain the situation, not wanting to embarrass her any more than he had already. He simply asked her to call him back.

No one returned his phone call though.

Alex ventured out for some lunch. He returned home and after eating, called Julieta a couple more times, each message more desperate than the last. The silence that followed was deafening and he could only wonder if he would ever talk to her, talk to them again.

When dawn broke the following morning, Alex was already awake. Though he still had a headache, the swelling in his face had gone down and the pain had subsided. He got ready for work, then drove over to Manny's house, as he did every day, praying the situation had settled.

Alex pulled up to the house and parked out front. Normally he would have blown the horn, but it didn't seem appropriate this morning. His palms sweaty and his head pounding, Alex got out, walked over to the door, and knocked. Then he waited patiently.

No response.

He knocked again, but like before, no one answered. Alex hopped off the front steps and walked over to the side of the house. Their car was gone, which meant Manny and Sonia were also gone. What about Julieta, though? Was she home? Or had she started school? He recalled how vehemently she argued against it. And if she hadn't, did he dare stay, hoping she would answer? Somehow, he didn't think she would.

Disappointed, Alex returned to his car and continued onto work. He didn't see Manny as he pulled into the hotel parking lot they were renovating, but the lights were on in the construction trailer. As the foreman, he was probably there. Alex grabbed his hard hat and tools from the backseat and ran over to the trailer to talk to him.

"What the hell happened to you?" a coworker asked him.

Alex didn't respond.

Inside the trailer, Manny was at his desk, going over paperwork. Alex approached him cautiously, his heart thundering in his chest. The man didn't acknowledge him though.

"Manny…," he said, his voice wavering. He cleared his throat and stood up straight, waiting for some form of recognition.

Manny didn't look up, just continued flipping through the papers.

"Listen," Alex started again, unsure of what he was going to say. What could he offer that Manny would accept?

The truth.

Alex cleared his throat again.

"Listen, Manny...about what happened..."

The man gazed up at him, his face hard, his eyes steely and black. Alex began losing courage, as he realized Manny had not even pondered forgiving him. But he couldn't back out. Not now.

"Manny, what happened between Julieta and I..."

His friend—former friend now—stood up and braced himself against the desk, menacingly. Alex took a step back.

"I think it was plain to see what was happening."

"It wasn't like that..."

Alex could hear the desperation in his own voice.

"Wasn't like what?" Manny asked, walking around the desk. Alex took another step back as the man stopped in front of him, the two now standing toe-to-toe. "You, trying to have sex with my sister? Is that what it 'wasn't'? And of course, you weren't taking advantage of her, right?"

"No—"

"She's a good girl, smart; she's going places, unlike you. You're a nobody who'd just hold her back."

"It wasn't like that...I care for her," Alex insisted, shaking his head.

"Because she revealed herself to you? How convenient. An easy lay, and if you can get her to believe your charade, she'll be your sure thing."

"No—"

"I'm saying this only once: you're gonna stay away from Julieta. Don't call the house, don't come near her, or I'll finish what I started."

Ruth E. Griffin

Sonia

"HOW WAS YOUR DAY?" SONIA ASKED Manny as he got in the car that evening.

"Same-old, same-old," he muttered as he buckled up his seatbelt.

She pulled out of the hotel parking lot and turned towards home. It had been a long day for her as well. As a high school teacher, she dealt with hormones and bad decisions all day, but worrying about how her husband dealt with Alex after a weekend of silence made the day that much worse. Manny didn't look like he had killed anyone, but she had to ask.

"Was he there?"

"Who?"

"Alex."

Manny gave her no response. He simply stared out the passenger window.

They had been married for eight years now, and though she could deal with most of his habits, his refusal to talk was the one that irked her the most. As a good wife, she usually gave him the space he needed to deal with his issues, but not today. The past few days had been miserable ones for everyone, and she wanted the situation resolved.

Sonia came to a red light and stopped. Then she punched him in his arm.

"*Conyo, mujer!*" he swore, rubbing his bicep. "What the hell is your problem?"

"You are," she retorted. "I asked you if he was there."

"Yes."

The disdain in his voice was as evident as his attitude.

"So...?"

"What?!"

"*Aye, Dios mio*," she cried. "Did you talk to him?"

"For what?"

He turned his attention to the road in from of them and turned his bottom lip up.

"You're really going to sit there and ask me that?" she cried.

"What do I need to say to him? He came in my house and tried to screw my sister. He's lucky I didn't kill him."

"You have to work with him. What are you going to do, ignore him?"

Manny didn't respond.

Sonia let it go…for now.

SONIA KICKED OFF her shoes and changed into something more comfortable when she got home. After washing up, she went to the kitchen to start dinner. She could hear Manny in the garage tinkering with his bike. It no longer worked, but because it was his father's, he didn't want to give it up.

As Sonia took out all the ingredients she needed to make *filete frito*, she thought back to when she first met Manny. They had grown up in the same neighborhood, attended the same schools and worshipped in the same church. Somewhere along the line though, their paths diverged. She studied hard to become a teacher and give back to her community, while Manny joined a gang and got into trouble. They saw each other coming and going and he would often hit on her and ask her out, but she always refused him. Sonia thought he was handsome, funny, and romantic. But also, arrogant and impetuous. She was not about to get involved with someone who could ruin her chances of making something of herself. He persisted though. So, she gave him an ultimatum: it was either her or his current lifestyle.

To her surprise, Manny 'quit' the gang—or distanced himself from it as much as he could. He cleaned himself up and got an honest job, making honest wages. He could still be cocky, but Sonia learned to overlook it. Love covers a multitude of sins, her priest had taught her, and regardless of how many faults they had, their love was enough to get them through it. Love, it seemed, was all they needed.

Then his parents died, leaving Manny with guardianship of Julieta. Sonia helped as much as she could, supporting her husband and caring for his sister. It was during this time that Manny matured into the responsible, caring man he was today.

Which made the current situation a contradiction: the man who had grown-up before her teetered on rage, while the child she had inherited was now a woman, hiding in shame. Sonia wanted to take their problems and fix them, but she knew it was unproductive to think like that. She had to be the voice of reason and get them talking—and forgiving—again. And if reason didn't work, she had to find something that did, something that drew them out of the shells they had buried themselves in. Sonia didn't have a game plan yet, but she was working on it. And once she came up with it, she knew she wouldn't have a problem with Julieta. She would listen. But Sonia wasn't so sure Manny would, considering his unwillingness to talk to Alex. Maybe it was because she was a woman, but in her mind, it seemed wrong that Manny was unwilling to hear him out. They had been friends for years; commuted together; hung out together; worked together. Alex had attached himself to the family and they had accepted him with open arms. Especially Julieta; while she never came out and told anyone how she felt about him, Sonia could see it in her eyes.

And knowing Alex as she did, Sonia found it hard to believe he would purposely take advantage of Julieta. Unfortunately, if they didn't speak to each other, they would never learn the truth about what happened. Or quite possibly, the fact that fate had brought them together.

Sonia smiled at the thought. Beyond Manny's cockiness and her strong will, fate had assigned them to each other. They belonged together—perhaps as much as Julieta and Alex did.

Sonia sighed; she was a hopeless romantic.

She turned her attention back to dinner preparation. She finished cooking, plated the food, and set the table. But when she called everyone in to eat, no one came. Julieta remained in her room and Manny in the garage. Sonia said nothing and ate dinner by herself. She had finished when Manny came in, smelling of gas and oil. He washed his hands, grabbed his plate, and sat in front of the television. Then Julieta came out of her room, leaning heavily on her cane. She had missed her physical therapy appointment and it was showing in her gait. She walked as far as the doorway between the kitchen and the living room, and announced, "I'm leaving."

Sonia's heart dropped. She didn't think Julieta was ready to move out, nor did she believe she was doing it because she wanted to 'spread her wings', so to speak. She was leaving because of Manny. Sonia turned to her husband to see how he reacted to the news, but he hadn't moved. He was still hunched over his plate, still eating as though she said nothing.

"I'm moving out next week with a friend of mine. Until then, I'll make myself scarce," Julieta continued. And though she spoke with resolve, Sonia could hear the sorrow in her voice.

Again, Manny said nothing, so she responded for him.

"*Mija*, you don't have to leave—"

"Let her go," Manny interrupted, still facing the television. "She's an ungrateful brat. Let her run away."

"Manuel! For God's sake—"

This time, Julieta cut her off.

"And you would know something about that, right?" she spewed towards her brother.

Manny stood up and marched over to her.

"I made mistakes, but I didn't run away. I have been here taking care of you and Sonia, working to put you through school, to put food in your mouth and a roof over your head.

You need to man up instead of blaming everyone else for *your* mistakes then running away."

"Why don't you man up!" Julieta exclaimed with unmasked indignation. "Whatever I did with Alex was my business, but you…all you do is boss me around, barge into my room, treat me like a child, like I don't have any sense or something."

"I think your little affair shows how much sense you don't have," Manny retorted. "Didn't I warn you? I said not to even look at guys like that. Told you not to trust them, but you gotta act like a bitch-in-heat—"

Julieta slapped him. Sonia usually didn't take sides, but a comment like that deserved no less of a response. It was uncalled for and childish and if Julieta hadn't slapped him, Sonia would have.

The two continued arguing, raising their voices until they were all that could be heard. At the end of her patience, Sonia got between them and pushed Manny back.

"*Basta!*" she yelled over their voices. "I am sick and tired of all this fighting!"

Manny glared at Julieta, who returned the sentiment.

"This has got to stop! If it's not one thing, it's the other. Regardless of what happened and who said what, you two cannot continue doing this."

The glares continued, until Julieta finally said, "I'm done. I'll be gone Saturday."

She turned around and limped back to her room.

Manny remained where he was standing, his ego wounded worse than his face. Sonia didn't dare say anything else, knowing she would only be inviting his wrath on her. Instead, she followed after Julieta as she returned to her room, and slammed the door shut. Sonia knocked several times, calling her sister-in-law's name, but she received no answer. She was ready to quit when the door opened, though just slightly. Sonia pushed it open the rest of the way and watched as Julieta hobbled into her room and took a seat on her bed. Taking this as an invitation, Sonia entered and shut the door behind her.

"Listen, *querida*, I know Manny can be a brute sometimes, but that's the only way he knows to express himself. It doesn't make it right, but you know how your brother is."

It wasn't her intention to excuse Manny's behavior, but Sonia had to start with something. Julieta didn't respond though. Sonia decided to go in a different direction.

"Your dinner is getting cold," she said.

"I'm not hungry," Julieta mumbled as she laid back on her bed and stared up at the light.

Sonia sighed.

"Do you mind if I sit with you?" she asked.

Julieta shrugged her shoulders.

Sonia sat beside her, then lay back so she was eye-to-eye with her sister-in-law.

"Do you want to talk?" she asked.

Julieta shook her head, still staring above her.

Sonia sighed, feeling helpless. She was always ready and willing to help, but things had changed so much since the accident, she didn't know what to say or do anymore.

Sonia reached over and smoothed Julieta's hair back. Though she had known her her entire life, it was only after the accident that she looked at her as her own. While she was okay co-parenting, Sonia only viewed her as Manny's sister, treating her as such and giving her freedoms she might not give her own flesh and blood. She obviously wasn't the motherly type; she was more career minded, with aspirations outside of the home. She wanted children, but the plan had always been to get to a good place financially before she and Manny started their family. Then the accident happened. Apart from the financial setback, Sonia became aware of an awakening of her maternal instincts; all she wanted was to protect Julieta from the bad things in the world.

She wasn't doing a good job.

"You have grown up into such a beautiful, smart woman," she told her.

Julieta scoffed at that.

"If I'm so smart, why did I fall for Alex's lies?" She finally turned to Sonia, her eyes glistening with tears. "I've had a crush on him for so long, but I never told anyone else. Why would I tell him, of all people?"

Julieta sat up. Sonia followed suit. She moved closer to her sister-in-law and wiped the tears that ran down her cheek.

"People react differently to anesthetics—"

"That's not what I mean."

Sonia sighed.

"We can't help who we fall for. Maybe in some subconscious way you wanted him to know. We're only human. We want those we love to love us back."

"I just can't believe he would do what he did." Her voice was broken, filled with pain. "I thought he was different, you know? I didn't care about his past. We all make mistakes. But I guess I was wrong. There's no fairy tale, no true love, not with men like that."

Sonia made a suggestion she knew Manny would not approve of.

"Why don't you talk to him? He's been calling and leaving messages for you."

"I don't want to talk to him. Or see him ever again."

"Will you at least reconsider leaving?"

Julieta shook her head.

"As long as I'm here, Manny's going to continue running my life, and I'm sick and tired of it. I can make my own decisions...," she said, "...even if they're bad ones."

Her voice trailed off into sobs. Sonia pulled Julieta into her arms and held her as she cried.

SONIA WAS UP late grading papers when Manny finally showered up and came to bed. His mood had improved enough to make him amorous, but she wasn't in the mood.

"Not tonight," she said brusquely and turned back to her papers.

Manny didn't persist but rolled over and was asleep in minutes.

Sonia stayed up a while longer before deciding to go to sleep too. She turned off the lights and lay back. The papers had been a temporary distraction. Now that the world was dark and quiet, all she had were her thoughts and they kept going back to Manny and Julieta and what she could do to help them.

Eventually Sonia fell asleep. Morning came with little fanfare—or much of anything else. Julieta and Manny got ready in silence. Neither said anything to the other, nor did they make eye contact. Sonia would have normally attempted getting them to talk to each other, but this morning, she didn't even try. The effort would not have ended well. Once she dropped them both off at their respective places, she drove to the high-school, where she taught tenth-grade English. It was a challenge on any normal day. Today, she found the task almost impossible. She was having trouble concentrating and was at a loss for direction.

Loss of control is more like it, she thought.

After lunch, her friend Celia, the music arts teacher, found her in her classroom, trying to reorganize herself. The woman was outgoing and engaging—*fun*, she often reminded Sonia, as she played salsa music and screened musicals in her classroom. This, of course, made her one of the more popular teachers, a distinction she lorded over everyone.

"I thought we were meeting for lunch," Celia said as she took a seat in a student chair across from Sonia's desk.

"I'm sorry," Sonia exclaimed. "I forgot."

Celia offered her a sympathetic smile.

"Things still bad at home? Anybody talking yet?"

"Not unless you count yelling as talking."

"Maybe in my house, but I guess that's not normal in yours, huh?"

"That's all they do now, and it's gotten worse since Friday."

Celia smiled knowingly and let out a drawn-out whistle.

"*Hermanita* getting it on with the *gringo*."

Sonia rolled her eyes. She and Celia were the same age, but the woman was, at times, immature.

"Celia—"

"What? I didn't know she had a thing for white boys—"

"Stop."

"They're not usually my type, but Alex is a looker, so I can understand the attraction—"

"Are you done?"

"Still though, if I caught my sister with a thug like that, I would have beat his ass too. I'm not saying fathead was right. I'm just saying."

Celia didn't like Manny and often referred to him by *other* names.

"Be nice," Sonia insisted, "And Alex is not a thug. You've met him, he wouldn't hurt a fly."

Celia shook her head, as if disappointed by Sonia's assessment of the young man.

"That's right, you have a soft spot for gang-bangers," her friend replied, though her tone remained playful.

"Stop it. This is serious. Julieta is gonna move out at the end of the week."

"She's not a little kid anymore, she's grown up."

"I know."

Celia stood up and walked over to Sonia's desk. She leaned on the corner and glared at her friend.

"Don't take this the wrong way, but I don't think you do. Ever since the accident, you've been…different."

The pitch of her voice had changed: she wasn't playing anymore.

"Different how?"

"I know you've always been a bit of a control freak, but lately, you've been obsessed with making sure everyone is okay. Whether it's Manny and Julieta or Alex and Julieta or you and Julieta."

"They're my family. Why wouldn't I?"

"Because it's not your responsibility to make things better for everyone. I didn't say anything before because I didn't think I'd have to. You've always been the smarter one. But that accident? It was *just* an accident. Regardless of who was driving, no one was at fault. Except the dumbass who ran into you. He was at fault, not you. From your perspective, though, it was *just* an accident and there is nothing you have to atone for. So, stop trying to fix everything."

Sonia wasn't stupid, she knew what she was feeling was guilt. But there was little she could do to get beyond it. So, she continued trying to control the uncontrollable, which only fed the culpability. She was a literal catch-22, and it was killing her.

"I can't sit back and do nothing," she finally admitted.

"You also can't control what other people do," her friend quietly reminded her.

"What am I supposed to do then?"

"Recognize the only person you need to fix is you."

"I can't do that."

"Okay, then treat them like the grown-ups they are."

"They're not listening to each other."

"Let them make their mistakes."

"And what if their mistakes are catastrophic?"

Celia sighed in resignation.

"You're gonna keep arguing with me, aren't you?"

"I'm not arguing—"

"Alright, then. Make the *sinvergüenza* fix this. It was his stupid ass that made this worse by beating up the poor guy. You take care of you and let him handle this."

Sonia frowned.

"You just told me to stop trying to fix things. Why is it okay for him to do it?"

"Honestly, I don't care what he does. I just know I lost my friend in that accident and I'd like to get her back."

SONIA DROVE INTO the parking lot of the construction site and put the car in neutral. She didn't have to pick up Julieta, as she was fortunate enough to find a ride home with a friend (presumably the one she was moving in with), but that left Sonia stuck waiting. It would be a few more months before they had enough saved up for another vehicle. Alex's willingness to give Manny rides home had freed up her schedule; and she missed being able to go home directly after school.

Focus, chica, she told herself.

Instead, her mind wandered as she waited. She thought about Celia. About Manny. About Julieta. About her life. And like a vice she wasn't supposed to indulge in, she looked around her, and thought about kids. She was still young enough to have them without complication, but it felt like lately her maternal clock was ticking louder and louder. Every time she brought up the subject with Manny, though, he was quick to dismiss it, telling her the time wasn't right. But no amount of planning could make the time right—the accident had shown them that. So why put off having kids any longer? She thought, then sighed. Sonia knew eventually Manny's answer would change, but she wasn't sure she could wait that long.

Choosing not to think about it, or her disappointment, Sonia instead focused on helping Julieta and making things easier for her, which made her wonder if that's what being a mother would like. Or was she trying to alleviate her guilt? Sonia was sure it was both; and the more she thought about it, the more she knew Celia was right. She was spreading herself thin and if she didn't stop, she was going to collapse under the weight she was trying to carry. Sonia needed to take care of herself as much as she was trying to care for everyone else.

Manny finally finished working and joined her at the car. He was quiet when he got in and didn't respond when Sonia asked him about his day. He only shrugged his shoulders and grunted something of a response.

He wasn't ready to talk.

Okay, she thought with frustration and remained silent for the rest of the trip. She held out hope that he would say something later, but when they arrived home, Manny disappeared into the garage to work on his bike. He didn't offer a word to her or his sister, who was in her room with her door shut. Sonia wanted to be sensitive to whatever was going on with him, but she had reached the end of her rope. She was ready to explode…but being the person she was, Sonia chose to remain calm.

Just let it go and fix dinner.

Sonia perused the fridge, looking for ideas for what to feed everyone. Then it hit her: what was the point of doing that when she had been eating dinner by herself all week? Manny and Julieta were both adults and could fend for themselves. This meant she was now free to do whatever her heart desired. The thought was enticing, especially when she looked at the time. She could watch her favorite *telenovela*. Yes, Sonia was serious and practical most of the time, but she also had a love for sappy, Latin soap operas that played on the heartstrings. She grabbed the tub of ice cream from the freezer and sat down on the couch. It had been a while since she last saw it, but she quickly caught up with the storyline and became engrossed in the lives of the characters once again.

Eventually Manny came in from the garage.

"Where's dinner?"

"I didn't cook," Sonia said, her eyes glued to the television.

"Why not?"

"I'm watching my story," she replied, matter-of-factly, as if this was something she did on a regular basis.

"What am I supposed to eat?"

"I don't know. Look in the fridge."

He clicked his tongue, annoyed.

"I work hard for you and Julieta. It'd be nice to have something hot and ready to eat."

Sonia could hear the reproach in his voice, and she was instantly irritated. But she was determined to stay calm. She stood up and faced him.

"I work all day too. And I'm happy to come home and cook dinner for you both, but what's the point? I cook by myself; I sit down by myself, and I clean up by myself. Then when you bother to stick your head in, all you do is fight with Julieta. That has been our lives since the accident and I'm tired of it."

Manny frowned.

"Where is all this coming from?"

Sonia wasn't sure if she should be upset with him, or try to reason with him, since her argument could be mistaken for sudden. Taking the higher road, she took a deep breath and said, "I don't know what to do anymore, Manny. I was talking to Celia today and she said—"

Her words trailed off when she saw Manny roll his eyes, his disdain for Celia as obvious as Celia's dislike for him.

"That woman doesn't know what she's talking about," Manny stated.

Sonia pursed her lips and put her hands on her hips. Her calm exterior was beginning to break.

"She's my friend."

"She's putting things in your head."

"You don't even know what she said."

"I've got some idea, based on your little outburst tonight."

Little?

Still trying to be the bigger person, Sonia bit her lip to keep from lashing out at Manny. She sucked in a deep breath and said, "You're really going to say that? After everything we've been through?"

"She says stuff to get to me."

"Because everything is about you, right?"

"No, but obviously she said something if you decided to come home and not cook dinner."

"Well, maybe I'm done cooking dinner and doing everything around here if this is the appreciation I'm going to get."

"So, this is what then, another ultimatum? I do what you say, or you don't act like a wife anymore?"

Sonia was done being the bigger and better person. She stormed past him into their bedroom, grabbed his pillow and a blanket and returned to the kitchen, where she tossed them at him.

"What the hell are you doing?" he demanded.

"You're on the couch."

"I am the man of this house!" Manny argued.

"And?" Sonia said.

"And the man sleeps in his bed with his woman by his side."

She could hear the aggravated tone in his voice. Good—maybe now he would listen.

"Well, *this* woman is sleeping by herself on the bed *she* made. You are going to sleep on the bed *you* made," she exclaimed, pointing to the couch.

Manny narrowed his eyes and opened his mouth to argue, but Sonia didn't let him.

"I've excused your behavior, told Julieta that it was Manny being Manny. I gave you your space, left you alone, but you are so stuck on yourself, you don't see what you have. I don't know what's going on with you and you keep pushing me and everyone else away. You won't talk to me; all you do is argue with Julieta; and Alex! *Dios mio*! It doesn't make sense to me that you would accept him as a friend and trust him like a brother but then you beat him up and put him out without even hearing him. Maybe he made a mistake. Maybe there were extenuating circumstances we don't know about. Or maybe, *just maybe*, he actually cares for Julieta. So, he was a screw-up in his former life. You seem to have forgotten how much of a punk you were when you were his age. Still, I loved you and encouraged you to become the man I knew you had it in you to be. How do you know Julieta can't do that for him? She cares for him, you know. You just have to open up your eyes to see it. But no, you gotta be pig-headed and now she's leaving."

Sonia paused for a breath. Manny took advantage of her momentary silence to argue. "So that's what this is about? Just because I don't want to have kids yet, you're going to keep her at home?"

Angry at his insensitivity, Sonia grabbed his shirt and pulled him to her. Then she lowered her voice so that Julieta wouldn't hear what she had to say.

"This has nothing to do with that. Yes, I want her to stay, but not because you decided now's not a good time for kids. She's my *hermana* as much as she is yours. But the truth is that she still needs support, still needs physical therapy. Is her friend going to pick up that burden? Is she going to tell her that she's still beautiful, even with scars? Is she going to love her and encourage her to be her best, even when life changes? One day she'll be ready to move out on her own but right now, she's only going because of *you*; and the sad part is, you're too blind to see it!"

Manny

MANNY STOOD IN THE KITCHEN, wondering what the hell happened. He had asked one question, only to get into an argument. What was wrong with everyone? First Julieta, then Alex and now Sonia? They had all gone off the deep end, leaving him to fight for his sanity—and his dinner.

Angry and frustrated, Manny stepped over the items on the floor and stomped over to the sink. He washed his hands, then foraged through the refrigerator for something to eat. He finally decided on a bowl of cereal. This was no way for a man to end his day, but he was determined to show Sonia that he could function without her.

After eating, Manny grabbed his pillow and blanket and plopped down on the couch. He laid back and stretched his legs over the arm of the chair, trying to get comfortable. It didn't work. He hit the pillow and turned over on his side, but his frame was not made to sleep on the sofa. He blew out an angry breath—he wasn't going to be getting any rest tonight.

Not that it mattered. He was too busy stewing to even relax, much less sleep. Though he had the television on, he found it hard to concentrate on the programming. He couldn't get Sonia's words out of his head. What did she mean, he was blind because he chose to be? Manny had taken care of his sister since his parents died. She was all he had outside of Sonia, and he was all she had. What exactly had he missed?

Yes, they fought a lot lately, but it wasn't like he was shirking his duties. He clothed her, fed her, provided for her and protected her. So, to see her in bed with Alex, kissing and doing all sorts of adult stuff was more than he could handle. Perhaps his reaction was extreme, but in his mind, he didn't do anything his own father wouldn't have done. Even as rash as his actions were, Manny didn't regret them at all. He was Julieta's guardian; and if he did nothing else right, he would make sure she was safe from men like Alex. Whether she saw it or not.

IT WAS STILL dark outside when Manny woke up on the floor. Apparently, he had rolled off the couch at some point in the night and kept right on sleeping. He was suffering because of it now though: there was a kink in his neck and pain in his back. He had a string of obscenities ready, but first he had to get up. With much difficulty, Manny grabbed the side of the couch and slowly pulled himself up. His back cracked in various places, but he managed to get up on his feet and stretch.

It didn't help.

He shuffled to the bathroom to relieve himself then sat down on the recliner, knowing he would not be able to get back to sleep. He considered going to bed and letting Sonia know who the man of the house was, but he was afraid she would say she was.

Manny finally got up after a while and walked into the garage. He left the lights off as he expertly made his way over to his bike. It was basically beyond repair, but he couldn't bring himself to part with it. The motorcycle was the only thing he had left that connected him to his dad. Manny recalled the way the man took care of it, wiping it down daily and making sure everything was in working order. Even though it went against his mom's wishes, his father would take Manny and Julieta on rides through the neighborhood. It was a thrill Manny always looked forward to when he was younger—and one he took for granted as he entered his teenaged years. He lost track of what was important after that. Manny eventually found his way back, but he knew if he sold the bike now, he would lose the little bit of his father he had left.

With a tired sigh, Manny turned over an empty crate and sat down next to the bike. He was thinking about what he had to do to get it running again when the kitchen light suddenly came on. It was still early, but he knew it was Sonia, getting the coffee ready. He started to get up when he heard her talking with a hushed voice. He thought she might be talking to him, but then he heard Julieta respond. Manny sat back down and listened, remembering better times, earlier times, before the accident and everything that went to hell with it.

Though it had only been a few months, it felt like an eternity since the day their lives changed. Manny rushed to the hospital, certain he had lost both Sonia and Julieta. It wasn't until he received word that Sonia was okay that he began to relax and feel like he could handle what was happening. He was still anxious for Julieta but having Sonia by his side gave him a sense of wholeness that allowed him to step up and do what needed to be done. She was his better half, his best love. She had drawn out of him the man he had the potential to be—though apparently, he was failing in that department, if Julieta was moving out because of him.

He continued to replay Sonia's words: choosing to be blind? How? He saw Julieta for who she was: his little sister.

Julieta's soft laugh broke Manny out of his thoughts. He looked over to the doorway separating them and though he could only see part of her, he saw something he hadn't seen before: she had changed. Maybe it was the way she was sitting, carrying herself, or the way she was eye-to-eye with Sonia, drinking coffee and talking to her peer-to-peer. She wasn't the young child he had inherited—she had grown-up.

Manny wasn't sure why he was seeing this now. He wasn't stupid, he knew she was an adult. He had watched her go from a twelve-year-old girl to a twenty-two-year-old woman. He had seen her mature. He understood what that change was. He just couldn't get his brain to see her as anything other than that 'kid' he got stuck with.

He sighed. Okay, so he needed to admit Julieta was a woman. This still didn't excuse the fact that Alex had taken advantage of her.

Had he though? asked the accusatory voice inside his head.

What else could he have been doing? Manny had known him for years. They had welcomed him into the family, considered him one of their own, but not once had he said anything, had he shown any interest in Julieta.

Maybe because he was afraid of you.

Why would he be?

Did you see what you did to his face?

I was protecting Julieta.

Even so, Manny had to admit the young man was nothing but sincere. He had spent a couple of years in prison, but he was no longer that person. He treated Sonia and Julieta with respect. So, what happened? Why did he try to take advantage of Julieta? What changed?

The accident.

Everything kept coming back to that goddamned accident. It was as if everyone had changed because of it. Julieta suddenly didn't want to go to school. Sonia was acting strange, talking about kids and refusing to make dinner. And Alex? Since that day at the hospital, Alex seemed quieter, more observant, drawn to Julieta whenever he was over…

Dammit, Manny groaned. He hated when Sonia was right.

WHEN HE FINALLY emerged from the garage, Manny received a cold reception from Julieta. Without a word, she got up and walked out of the room. He supposed he deserved the treatment he was getting from her, but when he turned to Sonia, she simply handed him a cup of coffee, then left to shower.

There were no words between them as they got ready for the day and left for work. Silence was never an issue before today, but knowing he was partly responsible for the way everyone was feeling made him feel self-conscious and guilty. The feeling got worse when he walked into the trailer at work and saw Alex clocking in. He stopped in his tracks, stunned by the appearance of the young man's face. His eye was swollen, he had a cut across his cheek and his face was bruised purple and blue. Manny had seen the results of his actions many times in his past, but he had not felt any guilt over it.

Until now.

Alex turned around and saw Manny. The two made eye contact for a moment, before the younger man left the trailer, giving the older man a wide berth.

Manny cursed under his breath and proceeded towards his desk. He set his hardhat and tools down and took a seat. He looked around, trying to decide where to start, but knew he couldn't let the situation stay as it was. He needed to talk to Alex.

Before he could convince himself otherwise, Manny grabbed his hardhat and left the trailer. He searched the grounds, over by the food truck and the port-a-johns, but he didn't see Alex. Manny returned to the trailer and sat down. He didn't know what he was going to say anyway, so what did it matter?

Because you were wrong…

"Yeah, yeah, yeah," he mumbled to himself and went to look for Alex. After a floor-by-floor search of the hotel, he found him on the thirteenth floor. The man was working hard, tearing out drywall. Manny approached him, but when Alex saw him, he stopped what he was doing and stepped away from him. Manny remembered their last conversation and the promise he made. More reason to feel shame. But Alex knew he wouldn't follow through on his threat…right?

The bruises on Alex's face and his trepidation said otherwise, but what was Manny supposed to do? He couldn't take his words back—and part of him wasn't sure he wanted to. Not yet, at least. Not until he heard Alex's side of the story.

Manny stopped a few feet from him and cleared his throat.

"Listen," he began. "Last week was … crazy and I … overreacted. I mean this is Julieta we're talking about. She's the only family I got left. And I thought…well, that you had … do you understand?"

Alex said nothing. He didn't even make eye contact with Manny, just stared down at his feet. How was Manny supposed to apologize like this?

"Dammit," he muttered to himself, causing Alex to peer up at him. "Sorry. I didn't mean you. I mean, I don't apologize unless I'm wrong. And … I was, or my actions were over the top. I don't want there to be hard feelings between us."

Again, Alex's gaze was fixed on his shoe. What was so damn interesting down there?

"You can talk to me. Maybe we should talk. I mean, if this wasn't a one-time thing, then…this wasn't a one-time thing, was it? What you said—was it the truth? Or…"

Alex finally glanced at him, his face stoic.

Manny didn't know what else to say. This was not the reaction he imagined from Alex, but after the way he treated him, he knew he shouldn't expect anything less.

Uncomfortable with the situation, Manny tried to find a way to extricate himself.

"Are we cool man?"

Alex was quiet to the point of awkwardness. Finally, he said, "I gotta get back to work." And without waiting for a response, returned to what he was doing when the older man approached him.

Manny didn't know what else to do, so he returned to the trailer and focused on his own work until Sonia picked him up that evening. Manny couldn't tell if she was still upset with him, but she was quiet, which never boded well for him. She usually asked him about his day, while he let her carry the conversation. Listening to the silence between them made him realize how much he didn't talk. He wasn't even sure what to say now. So, he said nothing.

Julieta was sitting on the couch when they got home. She was working on her school-work, having started class as he had asked.

No, as he *told* her to. She obeyed him, but he hadn't stopped to listen to her and find out why she didn't want to go back. And now she was leaving. His actions would have killed his mother if she wasn't dead already.

With a sigh, he placed his hardhat and belt on the table and approached Julieta. He had struck out with Alex, perhaps he could garner her forgiveness.

Julieta, however, cut the television off when she saw him enter the room. With a tight lip and a hard face, she gathered her books, grabbed her cane and stood to her feet.

"Hold on, I want to talk to you," he said.

Julieta sneered at him, then tried to walk past him. He put his arm out to stop her.

"I said wait, I want to talk to you," he repeated, suddenly annoyed.

"Why don't you try asking?" she snapped at him.

Manny ground his teeth.

"Can I talk to you, Julieta? Please?"

She glared at him, as if considering the request.

If she says no...

But she didn't, just sat back down, looking everywhere but him.

Manny remained standing, but then thought better. He should be on her level, eye-to-eye, peer-to-peer—that's what he learned in his management training. Surely it was applicable here, even if it was brother-to-sister. He dropped into the chair beside her.

"Look," he began "I…was…I jumped the gun and did and said stuff… I didn't mean…" Manny struggled to come up with the right words. He didn't have to give her a long speech. He only had to offer her the one word she needed to hear—sorry. Manny was a proud man though and that word didn't roll off his tongue, often or easily.

"Are you done yet?" Julieta impatiently interjected.

"No!" he stated, trying to remain calm. "I'm trying to apologize, dammit."

"Well, you're doing a crappy job."

Manny fought everything in him not to snap at her.

"This isn't easy, you know."

"Neither is living under the same roof with you."

"I'm doing the best I can here, okay?"

At that, Julieta stood up and started out of the room. Manny instinctively followed her. He grabbed her arm to stop her, but she only pulled loose.

"Leave me alone," she insisted. "I'm done listening to your pathetic excuse of an apology. You're not sorry, you just want your wife to take you back to bed."

Manny was stunned silent for a moment, before getting his bearings and retorting, "That's out of line, *chica*."

Though she wasn't wrong.

"So was what you did last week," she exclaimed and pushed past him out of the room. He didn't follow. There was no point: she wasn't going to listen to him.

Manny turned back to the kitchen to get his gear and saw Sonia standing in the doorway, glaring at him. There was no judgment in her countenance, just sadness, like she understood what he was only starting to realize—that he had lost his family.

FLOWERS IN HAND, Manny wandered through the halls of the hospital, looking for Gary's room. The visit was overdue, but he had talked to the man's wife earlier that day and let her know he was coming to see him. The accident had snowballed into meetings, safety reviews and mandatory training for Manny and his crew; and while he understood the necessity of it all, he hated having to deal with any of it.

Of course, it was nothing compared to what Gary was dealing with. The man had a shattered pelvis and several broken limbs. His recovery would take months, if not years. Comparatively speaking, Manny had nothing to complain about.

After walking around for a few more minutes, he eventually found Gary's room and quietly knocked on the closed door, in case the man was asleep.

A woman's voice answered.

"*Adelante.*"

Manny entered the room, holding the flowers up. Gary, an older white man with a receding hairline, was lying in bed, the lower half of his body and right arm in casts. His face bore cuts and scratches from the pile of wood he landed on, and his body was bruised all over. Gary was in bad shape, but incredibly, he was smiling and laughing. No doubt because of the middle-aged Latin woman at his bedside, lovingly caring for him. Both glanced up at him as he approached the bed. Manny acknowledged her.

"*Señora,*" he said with a nod. Then plastered a forced smile on his face as he peered at Gary. "Hey man."

"Hey boss," Gary said. "Thanks for coming by."

"Sorry I couldn't make it sooner. Car issues."

Manny had borrowed a company vehicle to make this trip, pushing back the time that Sonia needed to pick him up. He felt bad knowing she would have to go back out to get him, but such was the nature of the situation until they could afford another car.

Gary nodded understandingly and introduced the woman.

"Carmen, this is Manny, my boss. His sister was in the accident, remember?"

She smiled sympathetically and asked, "How is she?"

Manny felt uncomfortable being the center of attention when it should clearly be on Gary.

"She's doing much better, thank you."

"I'm glad. It gives me hope for my Gary," she said. "Please tell her we're still praying for her."

Manny nodded. Carmen turned to her husband, kissed his lips, and smoothed out his hospital gown.

"I'm gonna head home for the night, *querido*."

"You don't have to go," Manny said. "I wasn't going to stay long."

"No, I was getting ready to leave. Stay," she told him. Then she turned to her husband and said, "Don't you go anywhere, okay?"

"I'll be right here, *mi amor*," he replied, his Spanish rough, but endearing. They kissed again.

Manny looked away, embarrassed. Apparently, he was beginning to make a habit of interrupting intimate moments between two consenting adults. He focused on the television until Carmen finished saying her goodbyes. Then he smiled politely at her as she walked by him, touching his arm as she did.

"She's a great woman," Gary stated, clearly in love.

Manny nodded yet again, uncertain of what he should say. He didn't know the woman, so it wasn't like he could argue the point. Not that he wanted to. He was sure she was great and so much more.

Focus!

Manny cleared his throat and his mind and said, "You're looking good." He was lying, but he couldn't say otherwise.

"Thank you."

He remembered the bouquet of flowers in his hands.

"These are for you. I didn't want to come empty-handed," he said.

"I appreciate that," Gary said, genuinely grateful for the gesture. He reached for them with his left hand but was hampered by the body cast. Manny wanted to kick himself for not being more considerate.

"Sorry. Here, I'll put them in water."

He looked around him and spotted a plastic tub by the sink. He wasn't sure what it was for, but it was clean and empty. Manny filled it up with water, placed the flowers in it and set them on the tray beside Gary's bed. The man gazed at them appreciatively.

"So, are they taking good care of you here?" Manny asked.

"The best."

"That's good. Any of the other guys stop by?"

"Yeah. A bunch of them were here earlier. It was good seeing them. They brought me some fried chicken. Food never tasted so good."

Again, his attitude was unbelievably positive, considering the situation he was in.

"I've gotta say, you are really taking this well."

"How can I complain when I'm still alive? No, regardless of what things look like, life is good."

Manny chuckled. "So are your meds," he quipped.

Gary laughed with him, but there was something in his eyes that went much deeper than the momentary mirth.

"Yes, they are, and I'm especially thankful for those right now. But the way I see things, everything could have been worse. Yeah, the accident was bad, but it wasn't fatal. I've got a few broken bones, but they'll eventually heal.

And regardless of the pain, I've learned what's truly important in life. Accidents like these make you re-examine yourself; they change you. Not because the things around you change, but because you change in response to them. All the regrets and fights and guilt you dealt with before—those things don't matter anymore, because you're alive and you've got a second chance to do and say things you should've done or said before. You know what I'm saying?"

Manny did. He absolutely did. And hearing Gary talk now made him realize what he needed to do to fix his family.

"THIS IS A stupid idea," Gary insisted, his outlook no longer positive. "Sonia's gonna kill you. Then she's gonna kill me for going along with it."

After much wheeling and cajoling, Manny convinced Gary to call Sonia and Alex and let them know Manny had been in an accident. After all, his reasoning went, if Julieta's accident had changed them, then another would do the same thing...

Right?

Of course it will, Manny chastised himself. *Think positive. This idea is nothing short of genius and it will save the day.*

Then Gary hung up the phone. The situation didn't seem as brilliant as it did a minute earlier.

This is a mistake, Manny thought. A big, catastrophic one. Sonia would not take the deception lightly; and after everything they had been through, it seemed like a selfish and cruel thing to do to her and to the rest of them. But he saw no other way to get their attention. Alex wasn't talking to him, Julieta wasn't listening, and Sonia was indifferent. Manny just hoped it wasn't too late.

Stop being negative. This is a good idea. It'll work out fine.

"This is a really, stupid idea," Gary reminded him, again. "I can't believe you talked me into helping you."

Manny shook his head, as he paced the floor.

"It'll work," he responded. "You'll see."

Even he wasn't convinced by his argument, but it was too late now to take it all back. He could only hope it worked. And if it didn't, then he was in the right place for all the pain they would inflict on him.

God, this was beginning to sound like the plot of one of those stupid *telenovelas* Sonia watched.

Manny took a seat beside Gary's bed and tried not to watch the clock. They'd be here soon enough and then he could explain himself. He turned the television on and sat back, searching the channels for a game to watch. It occurred to him then he was in Gary's room.

"You good with a game?"

Gary appeared almost amused by the question, as if it was the last thing Manny should be worried about.

Manny continued channel surfing. He instinctively looked up at the clock, then back down when he realized what he was doing.

"This is not going to work," Gary ventured once more.

"It'll work," Manny stated, though he was starting to waver in that conviction. Still, he couldn't let his doubt show.

This will work. It has to, he told himself, squaring his shoulders and straightening his back.

Gary shook his head but said nothing.

The time continued its glacier pace. Manny grew tired of the television. His leg started bouncing. He needed to get up and walk around.

Then he heard Sonia's worried voice echo into the doorway of Gary's room.

"Manny!"

She rushed in, her pace frantic, her face a mixture of worry and fear. Then she saw him, standing whole and uninjured, inches from the bed he was supposed to be occupying. She stopped cold in her tracks and demanded, "What the hell is going on?"

Gary pursed his lips and glowered at Manny, as if to say, 'I told you.'

"What the hell...?" she asked again, her confusion quickly morphing to rage. She advanced towards him, her demeanor menacing. Manny instinctively stepped back. He might have been a sight to behold in his anger, but she was more frightening than he could ever be.

"*Querida,* listen," he began, but she didn't let him finish.

"What is this? What the hell is going on?"

She drew closer to him, as he stepped further away from her.

"Let me explain," he tried, but she wasn't listening. Instead, she had removed her purse from her shoulder and was hitting him with it.

"Is this your way of getting back at me? Is that it? You want attention?"

"No, listen—"

"Poor little Manny, always gotta be the center of attention. And you…"

She turned her attention to Gary, whose eyes widened to the size of saucers. Manny immediately grabbed her around the waist and pulled her back away from him. He would never be able to explain what happened to Gary to the man's wife if Sonia got to him.

"What kind of sick game are you two playing?" she demanded.

But Manny didn't get a chance to respond. A confused voice interrupted them.

"What's going on?"

Manny stopped fighting Sonia and turned towards the door where Julieta stood, leaning on her cane, the expression on her face teetering between confusion and anger. Understanding dawned on her as she realized the whole situation was a sham. That wasn't what Manny intended. He simply wanted to get everyone in the same room to talk. Going by what he saw on her face though, this wasn't going to happen. He had lost her for good if he couldn't find a way to fix this.

It seemed Sonia had the same idea, for she had pulled from Manny's hold and was moving towards her sister-in-law. But in the time it took her to say her name, Julieta did an about-face and started out of the room. Manny pushed past his wife, no longer willing to allow his sister to leave or his wife to pick up his slack.

"Wait," he yelled.

But she didn't. She was halfway out the door and into the hallway before he reached her. Though he hated to manhandle her in her current state, he grabbed her arm and pulled her towards him. She almost lost her balance, but Manny caught her and steadied her.

"Let me go!" she yelled, drawing looks from nearby patients and nurses.

"Please, let me explain," he begged, but she pulled and wriggled in his arms, trying to get out of his grip. Understanding that he was not going to be able to hold onto her without making a scene, Manny released her and took a step back away from her. She resumed her escape.

"I was an ass. I'm sorry," Manny said quickly, hoping to get her attention.

She took another step away from him.

"The truth is, ever since the accident, I've been trying to make up for all my regrets. For every bad decision I've made. For disappointing *Mami* and *Papi.* For not being a better brother to you." Manny had thought the words would be bitter if he ever said them, but they weren't. They stung certainly; but he felt…lighter now. He continued. "I thought if I pushed you to do better than I did, then maybe it would make up for all everything I didn't do. And you would never experience the regrets I did."

Julieta stopped.

"I couldn't see beyond myself, and I pushed you away. I don't want you to go. Not like that. You're my sister."

He took a couple of steps towards her and stopped. Manny wanted to take the conversation back into the room, but he didn't want to scare her, or push her away either. He had no choice but to wait.

After a couple of minutes, Julieta turned around and looked up at him. Her lips were pursed, and her eyes narrowed, but the rage that had clouded them moments earlier was gone.

"I'm sorry it took me so long to see this," Manny added. "And to apologize."

He stepped closer to her. She didn't walk away.

"Will you forgive me?"

He put his arms around her and hugged her. For a moment, he was the only one expending any effort. Then he felt her arms wrap around him. He held onto her as long as she let him. When she finally let go, Manny looked down at his sister, as if seeing her for the first time. He meant everything he said, regardless of how hard it was to say, and he hoped she understood that.

The smirk on her face said she did.

"You're an idiot," she said.

He put his arm around her and turned her back in the direction of the room. He was done performing for everyone.

"I know. But you still love me."

"Only because I have to."

"Will you stay? We'll talk about school and setting up boundaries—for me."

Harder words were never uttered.

"Yeah," she said.

Sonia was standing at the door, waiting on them. She offered him a small smile as she took Julieta's hand in hers. He let her go and watched as they walked back into the room. Even Gary appeared happy for them.

But it was too early to call it a victory. Even though Manny had cleared things up with Julieta, he still needed to talk to Sonia and then there was the question of Alex.

"Why didn't you just call a family meeting or something? Why scare us?" Sonia asked.

"Well, there was another part to this, but it seems maybe I screwed that up beyond repair," he replied honestly. Alex had not shown up and given that he lived closer to the hospital than they did, it seemed unlikely that he would.

"And what was that?" Sonia asked.

Manny started to answer, but then he saw Julieta's eyes go wide and he heard her breath hitch. He looked behind him. Alex was standing in the doorway, his countenance marked by confusion. Manny didn't wait for him to react as Julieta did. He approached Alex before he could think about leaving, but like before, the man stepped back.

Manny stopped, aptly humbled. Alex's reaction to him was well-deserved, but the fact that he had showed up to the hospital meant he still cared for him and might be willing to listen.

"I'll explain everything in a minute," Manny began, "I want to apologize first for how I behaved. I shouldn't have jumped on you the way I did. You've been like a brother to me, and I should have trusted you. I'm sorry."

Alex looked down, his face flushed with embarrassment. Manny didn't consider his reaction as he hastily put his plan together. The younger man hated being the center of attention and often shunned it. But since

Manny publicly humiliated him, it was only right Manny publicly apologize.

Like Julieta though, Alex offered no response. In fact, he wouldn't even look at Manny, though he did glance at Julieta, before looking back down. Manny turned to his sister to see that she too had looked away. It wasn't his business to get in the middle of whatever was it they had. But since he interfered, he had to make this right as well.

Manny sighed. He was going to have to make sure he never screwed anything else up in his life—he hated apologizing.

He walked over to his sister and took her hand. She looked up at him with apprehension and aptly so, because he intended for her and Alex to talk and square things up. They might walk away from each other, but they would do so after clearing the air first.

Manny started to walk her over to Alex, but she resisted and tried to pull away from him. He didn't let up though. He took her step-by-step until she was standing in front of Alex, who had an equally apprehensive expression on his face.

"Look," Manny started. "I got in the middle of something that was none of my business. I should have trusted you two to…"

Do what? It was pretty obvious what they were doing; and to be honest, the thought of his little sister doing those things was enough to make him want to pummel someone else. But she was a woman, a beautiful one, smart too; and entitled to love, if this is what the situation was.

"I should have trusted you two to work things out on your own. So…" Again, struggling for words, Manny waved his hands in front of him, as if by doing so, he was transferring responsibility of the situation to them. "Work it out."

He stepped back and allowed the two their space. But neither looked at each other, nor did they say anything. They kept their heads down and their tongues silent.

Damn, tough audience.

Manny was considering what he could say to jumpstart the conversation when he noticed Julieta's lips purse, and her eyes narrow. She was still angry with Alex and was about to unleash her wrath on him.

"What exactly did I say while I was *under the influence* of anesthesia?" Julieta asked, her words pointed and deliberate, her tone cold and bitter. She put a heavy emphasis on her state of mind at the time, reminding everyone that she was the victim in all this.

Alex looked up at Julieta and frowned, unsure he wanted to honor her request. Even Manny wondered if it was a smart one. She was humiliated when Alex only alluded to what she said. Wouldn't the actual confession make it worse?

Julieta didn't back down though. She met Alex's gaze and glared at him until it became uncomfortable for everyone in the room. He sighed with resignation and in a low voice, broadcasted, "You said, 'Alex. I know I'm not perfect, beautiful, or anything important, and you would never want me, but I think about you every day. You take my breath away. I go to sleep thinking about you, and I wake up smiling because I may see you. If you gave me one chance, I'd show you how amazing we could be. I love you.'"

Manny cringed as Alex spoke, but worse still was watching Julieta's face redden with each word. She darted her eyes away from him but there was no change in her expression. It remained hard.

"Why did you believe me?" she demanded.

Alex hesitated, glancing around at everyone else in the room. He wanted out of the situation, but Manny could see Julieta wasn't going to let him slide by without answering.

"No," she said, "Everyone knows how I feel, and I had no say in that, so you don't get to be quiet on this. Why did you believe me?"

Alex shook his head, avoiding her gaze now as she avoided his just moments earlier.

"I don't know," he said. "I guess after everything I've done, I didn't think I was good enough for someone like you. Maybe knowing you *felt* about me the way you did gave me hope that I was worthy of something better." The pained expression on Alex's face was enough to make Manny uncomfortable. "I know I should have said something, but I didn't want you thinking that was the only reason I was with you."

Julieta scoffed at him.

"But it was."

"Maybe," he agreed, then seemed to change his mind. "No… I don't know…," he added with less assurance. "It was the reason I kissed you the first time, but not the second time and every time after that. I fell in love with you."

The words caught everyone by surprise. Manny was astounded to hear him admit something most men waited on their partner to say first. Gary watched with renewed interest, while Sonia took everything in with the same fervor as she did her *telenovelas*. Even Julieta's expression changed from hard to curious.

"I love you," Alex reiterated as he made eye contact with her. "Maybe it took you saying what you said for me to see that, but it's true. I want to be with you. I want to spend time with you. I want to make you happy. I'm sorry for putting you through everything I did. I should have told you, I get that. If I could go back and do things right, I would, but I can't and if you choose not to forgive me, I understand. I just ask, if you don't believe anything else, know that there's no way I would have taken advantage of you. Not before for Manny's sake and not now for yours. You were the best thing in my life, and I would have never hurt you like that."

The embarrassment was gone from Alex's face, but not the uncertainty of what would be. He looked to Julieta for some kind of reaction, but she offered none, good or bad. She simply watched him, studying his face for anything that contradicted what he was telling her. Silence abounded, interrupted only by the sounds of the television.

After a few moments, Julieta finally cleared her throat, though her the expression remained stoic. She didn't say anything but began closing the space between them. Alex eyed her carefully, now scrutinizing her as she had done him. He let his shoulders relax some as Julieta stepped in from of him, but remained guarded, even as she cupped his bruised cheek softly, rose up on her toes and kissed him on the lips. Alex simply watched her though.

"Why did you do that?" he asked, quietly, when she finally pulled away.

Julieta smirked and replied, "Because I care about you."

A smiled appeared on his face, and he leaned down and kissed her, pulling her towards him.

Manny watched the two with a lighter heart. He may not have understood what occurred between them just now, but he understood the emotions Alex had expressed. His love for Sonia may not have started accidentally, but it was the very thing that kept him going. And if their experience was any indicator, then Alex and Julieta were going to be alright.

Julieta was still his little sister though and seeing her with Alex was not something Manny was ready for yet.

"Hey, hey, hey, stop that," he insisted. "I don't care if you two are in love, you are never going to be alone as long as I'm breathing. Stop that—"

Sonia pulled the curtain that was hanging from the ceiling and divided the room in half, separating them from Alex and Julieta.

"Leave them. They're good kids."

"I don't know if I can do this. Accepting that she's grown up is one thing. Now she's got a boyfriend?"

At that, Sonia smiled, but she didn't argue back as he expected her to.

"You did good, *Papi*," she said softly and kissed him on the lips. It was a gentle peck, but it was filled with all the love she still felt for him, despite his actions.

"Will you forgive me?" he asked her.

"Yes, but don't ever do anything like that again or next time there you will require medical attention."

He laughed, even though her threat was a genuine one. Then he asked her the one question he knew meant more than anything else he had said. "You want to make a baby tonight?" He had pondered the argument since Sonia banished him to the couch and while it would get him back in his bed with his wife and in her good graces, he knew it was time they tried. In fact, he knew there would be no better time.

Sonia's eyes lit up.

"Are you serious?"

"You were right. About everything. I know that wasn't a very romantic way to tell you, but—"

She placed her hand to his mouth to quiet him.

"I don't need romantic. I just need you."

She kissed him again, this time longer and with more passion. They were lost in the moment, until Gary cleared his throat and spoke up.

"Hey guys…"

About the Author

Ruth E. Griffin began telling stories at a young age, first with pictures, then with words. Even though she always considered herself an artist first, Ruth has been writing since grade school. She penned her first book as a teenager and has continued writing since then. Ruth is now the award-winning author of several books, which center on women's experiences. She is the founder of Studio Griffin, LLC., a full-service hybrid press; as well as a cohost of Authors Up, a streaming radio show that provides a platform for new, established, and aspiring authors. A New Jersey native, Ruth now resides in North Carolina with her husband. They are parents to four adult children. Her books are available at all major online bookstores.

Ruth E. Griffin

www.ingramcontent.com/pod-product-compliance
Lightning Source LLC
Chambersburg PA
CBHW031028190726
48286CB00003BA/1067